candles

glow sticks

honor table

lantern

Asian pears

sticks for lanterns

picnic blanket

Thanking the Moon

Celebrating the Mid-Autumn Moon Festival

Grace Lin

Alfred A. Knopf New York

THIS IS A BORZOI BOOK PUBLISHED BY ALFRED A. KNOPF

Copyright © 2010 by Grace Lin

All rights reserved. Published in the United States by Alfred A. Knopf, an imprint of

Random House Children's Books, a division of Random House, Inc., New York.

Knopf, Borzoi Books, and the colophon are registered trademarks of Random House, Inc.

Visit us on the Web! www.randomhouse.com/kids

Educators and librarians, for a variety of teaching tools, visit us at www.randomhouse.com/teachers

Library of Congress Cataloging-in-Publication Data

Lin, Grace.

Thanking the moon : celebrating the Mid-Autumn Moon Festival / Grace Lin. — 1st ed.

p. cm.

Summary: Each member of a Chinese family contributes to the celebration of the Mid-Autumn Moon Festival.

Includes author's note explaining this festival's customs and traditions.

ISBN 978-0-375-86101-7 (trade) — ISBN 978-0-375-96101-4 (lib. bdg.)

[1. Mid-autumn Festival—Fiction. 2. Moon—Fiction. 3. Food—Fiction. 4. China—Fiction.] I. Title.

PZ7.L644Th 2010

[E]—dc22

2009052349

The illustrations in this book were created using gouache.

MANUFACTURED IN MALAYSIA

September 2010

10 9 8 7 6 5 4 3 2 1

First Edition

To Kieran Cappy Kendall

The mid-autumn moon glows in the sky.
We go into the night to admire it.

Ma-Ma prepares the nighttime picnic.

Ba-Ba arranges the moon-honoring table.

Mei-Mei plays with the pale green pomelo peel.

Jie-Jie brings out the glowing lanterns.

And I pour the round cups of tea.

We all eat soft, sweet mooncakes.

Then we thank the moon for bringing us together
and send it our secret wishes.

It peacefully watches over all of us . . .

. . . this night of the Mid-Autumn Moon Festival.

The Mid-Autumn Festival, also commonly called the Moon Festival, is the thanksgiving holiday for the Chinese and many other Asian peoples. Celebrated on the fifteenth day of the eighth lunar month (which, using the solar calendar, falls sometime during September or October), the holiday began as a harvest festival. It marked the time when farmers had finished gathering their crops. Now it is celebrated as a time to give thanks for a good year and to come together with family.

The traditions and myths of the Mid-Autumn Festival center around the moon. On the night of the festival, the moon is bright and full in the sky. The roundness of the moon symbolizes harmony, and its fullness symbolizes wholeness, so families come together to celebrate those virtues.

Families pay homage to the moon by eating mooncakes, small, round pastries with sweet fillings. The cakes are formed in molds, and have elaborate designs on top. Chinese characters for harmony or longevity, figures from moon legends, or flowers add to the mooncake's role as

a symbol of good fortune and blessing. Sometimes rice-flour sponge cakes or smiling steamed cakes accompany the mooncakes to symbolize prosperity. Moon-shaped fruits such as pomelos, grapes, and Asian pears, as well as round cups of tea, are also traditional foods of this holiday.

Children, allowed to stay up late, parade with lanterns in the moonlight. The paper lanterns are usually round like the moon or have the shape of animals, like rabbits (a white rabbit is said to live on the moon) or horses (the moon is said to move at a horse's pace). Children also peer into the sky, hoping to see Chang-O, the moon goddess, looking down at them from her palace on the moon. Adults sometimes read or recite moon-inspired poems. And everyone sends a secret, unspoken wish up to the moon with the hope that Chang-O will grant it.

The Mid-Autumn Festival remains a beloved celebration and, along with the Lunar New Year, is one of the most important holidays of the year. Just as the moon always returns to its fullness, the festival continues to reunite families and inspire peace and gratitude.

mooncakes

book of Chinese poetry

tea set

rabbit statue

smiling steamed cakes

pomelos